To Jennifer —
Thank you for your
stories!
Catherine

Catherine Temma Davidson

THE ORCHARD

Catherine Temma Davidson is the author of the novel *The Priest Fainted*, a "resonant mélange of wisdom and humor, a testimony to the strong bonds of family and cultural traditions" (*Publishers Weekly*). Her poetry has won acclaim on both sides of the Atlantic, including a 2016 commendation for the Troubadour International Poetry Prize. The grandchild of immigrants and an immigrant herself, Catherine teaches writing to international students and works as a writing consultant at Amnesty International. She serves on the board of Exiled Writers Ink, an organization that promotes writing by refug̶e̶e̶s̶ ̶a̶n̶d̶ ̶a̶s̶y̶l̶u̶m̶ ̶s̶e̶e̶k̶e̶r̶s̶.̶ ̶O̶r̶i̶g̶i̶-nally from Sout̶h̶e̶r̶n̶ ̶C̶a̶l̶i̶f̶o̶r̶n̶i̶a̶,̶ ̶s̶h̶e̶ ̶l̶i̶v̶e̶s̶ in London wit̶h̶

D1342501

First published by GemmaMedia in 2018.

Gemma Open Door
230 Commercial Street
Boston MA 02109 USA

www.gemmamedia.org

Printed in the United States of America
978-1-936846-64-1

Library of Congress Cataloging-in-Publication Data

Names: Davidson, Catherine Temma, 1963- author.
Title: The orchard / Catherine Temma Davidson.
Description: Boston, MA : GemmaMedia, 2018. | Series: Gemma
open door |
    Identifiers: LCCN 2017057318 (print) | LCCN 2017060904
(ebook) | ISBN
    9781936846658 (ebook) | ISBN 9781936846641
Subjects: LCSH: Immigrants--Fiction. | Greek Americans--Fiction. |
    Grandparents--Fiction. | GSAFD: Domestic fiction.
Classification: LCC PS3554.A9243 (ebook) | LCC PS3554.A9243
O73 2018 (print)
    | DDC 813/.54--dc23
LC record available at https://lccn.loc.gov/2017057318

Cover by Laura Shaw Design.

Gemma's Open Doors provide fresh stories, new ideas, and essential resources for young people and adults as they embrace the power of reading and the written word.

Brian Bouldrey
Series Editor

GEMMA

Open Door

To my family, on both sides

PROLOGUE

Apricot Jam

What is an apricot? An apricot is a small fruit, from a small tree. Apricots fit into your hand. They fit into your pocket.

Everyone knows about peaches. Peaches get good publicity. They appear on posters and in poems. Apricots are the poor relation of the peach, the cousin with only a suitcase. But when you eat an apricot, you understand its power.

The flavor is deeper, stronger. It comes alive on your tongue and bites. You can cook with apricots. You can dry them. Dried apricots keep their flavor like no other fruit. Apricots can be addictive.

Inside the apricot is a stone. Inside the stone is a soft heart. Inside the soft heart? Some say poison. Some say health. Eat too much and it can kill you. Eat just enough and it can cure you.

Where do apricots come from? China? India? People have been eating apricots for a long time. You can find traces of apricots in ruins three thousand years old.

The scientific name for the apricot is *Prunus armeniaca*, the Armenian plum. Today in Palestine if you say, "during apricot-blossom time," you mean "never." In Turkish, to say a thing is like "an apricot from Damascus" means there is nothing better.

There are many ways to make apricot jam. If you want a clear, sweet jam, it is easy. Find some lovely fruit. Take out the hard stones. Cut the fruit up into pieces. Put it into a big pot. Bring it to a boil. Add sugar. In ten to fifteen minutes, the fruit is cooked. Pop it into jars and voilà!

There is another way to make the jam, which I learned from my brother-in-law from Beirut. He learned it from his Syrian mother. Put the cooked apricots in pans. Use the pans your mother gave you. If you have lost your mother, buy new pans. Leave the pans in the sun. Cover them with cloth. The heat will pull up the water. Soon the fruit will turn the color of copper, of smoke. The taste deepens as the color darkens.

After a week, this jam will be ready for your jars.

When you eat this sun-ripened jam, part of you sings and part of you cries. You want to put spoonful after spoonful into your mouth until your belly hurts.

All the apricots in the world are linked to the first apricot. That piece of fruit came from a wild forest. One day, a human walking through the woods looked up. There in the branches was a glint of gold. Luckily for us, our ancestors knew how to climb. They knew how to reach. They knew how to grab for sweetness wherever they could.

CHAPTER 1

On the Road

Lisa Katsouris left Los Angeles to drive eighty-three miles north to the family orchard in Ojai. She was alone in the car. Alone was not what she had expected to be.

The first time Lisa had done this trip, she was a baby in the back of her parents' car. Fifty years later, her hands were on the wheel.

It was her grandfather Joe's hundredth birthday. His family was gathering to celebrate. Some lived nearby. Some were arriving from as far away as New York.

1

Lisa's grandfather bought the orchard in 1957, the same year Lisa was born. All her life, she had felt linked to those trees.

Joe Katsouris came to America in 1925. He was an orphan with an orphaned wife. Both Joe and Anna had been born Greeks in Turkey under the Ottoman Empire. They lost their families when a rise in nationalism broke up the old borders. Greece for the Greeks. Turkey for the Turks. Muslim Greeks were expelled from Greece and ethnic Greeks were forced out of Turkey. Many people died. Lisa's grandparents were among a million refugees who fled to Greece.

Joe and Anna met in a camp in northern Greece. They were too Greek for the Turks, but too Turkish for the Greeks. So they ended up in America. They settled in California, where they had four children. Joe and Anna worked so hard they never looked up.

Never looked up, according to Joe, until the day he saw a parcel of land for sale in Ojai. There were rows of apricot trees in blossom; there were poppies growing in the grass. The orchard reminded him of the world he had known at the beginning of his life, a world unbroken.

He bought the land. For years afterward, his family grew around him: children, grandchildren. They gathered every weekend, then every month. Eventually, they came once a year. Then Anna died. The generations scattered.

Still, his family came back when they could, from close by and from far away.

When Lisa had a daughter, Anya, she brought her, too. For twenty years, mother and daughter travelled to the orchard together. Lisa was a good gardener. She nurtured her daughter well. But now a blight had come between them.

How would she explain it to her family? She might have to lie. There was always a chance Anya would come on her own.

At midday the lanes of the highway were empty. Lisa had cleared her schedule to get ahead of the weekend crowds. She zipped through North Hollywood and most of the Valley.

At a place where three freeways came

together, the traffic slowed. Lisa shifted gears. The early-summer sun muscled through the June gloom. Soon she was out of the suburbs and racing into the open hills near Thousand Oaks.

Already, the spring grass had dried to gold. The hills shone under blue skies. The road dropped into the farmland and beach towns of Ventura County. Soon the ocean appeared, glittering like a blue bowl filled with crystals.

All week, she'd felt like a trapped bird, beating against the glass. Now she was flying. Why let the fight with her daughter weigh her down?

She put on one of her favorite songs from when she had been Anya's age. Jackson Browne was her teenage crush, with his long hair and soulful eyes.

He sang: "Running on, running on empty," and she sang along.

No one was there to stop her. No one could sink against the seat and say, *You are so embarrassing.*

"Running wild!" she let herself howl.

A large white truck came up behind her. It sat on her tail. Lisa saw the driver in her rearview mirror. He wore dark sunglasses and a cap. They were in the middle lane. He wanted her to move. Instead, she slowed down.

He inched closer. She slowed more. She could feel his temper rising. Lisa's rose, too. They played psychological warfare. Finally, the other driver swerved. His truck zoomed ahead in a screech of tires.

That was fun, she thought. What would Anya have said?

Don't, Mom. Don't! He's probably got a gun. She heard Anya's voice in her head, louder than any music. She imagined her own reply: *Guns and trucks! Each his own personal Wild West! These people have ruined California!*

Then she thought about the real words her daughter had spoken the week before, words she wished she could block out: "You like to fight! You look for enemies! But it's turned you into a bigot. I can make a different choice."

Oh, Anya.

CHAPTER 2

A Beautiful Vision

When Lisa was a teenager, she often got angry with her own parents. Her mother, Claire, was French-Canadian. Claire had dyed-blond hair and had been a cheerleader for the UCLA basketball team. Her father, Jack, was Joe's oldest son.

Jack Katsouris had been a star shooter and an A student at UCLA. He worked hard. In 1955, he was the only ethnic on the basketball team. Lisa's parents were outsiders who wanted to be insiders.

Jack and Claire were Californians: cheerful and upbeat. Jack was a lawyer, like Lisa. Unlike Lisa, he never lost his temper or his cool. Her mother loved being a housewife. As a girl, Lisa thought her parents were boring. She was fascinated by her grandparents.

Americans are only interested in two tenses: present and future. Her foreign grandparents brought a past with them. When she was around her father's family, life took on a deeper flavor. Loss was part of happiness, bitter mixed with sweet.

The difference between her parents and her grandparents was the difference between American and Greek Easter. The first was pretty, pink and green: bunnies, hats, tulips, and sugar. In school and on TV, this was the official Easter.

But the real Easter happened on

a different day. Her extended family joined her grandparents at the Greek Orthodox church in Ventura. The service began at ten p.m. The priests sang with real grief and real joy in an ancient language. They swung incense through the night air. The faithful lit candles that sometimes burned Lisa's hair. The family kept the candles with them, carrying them in their cars to Joe and Anna's house. They ate their feast after midnight. The soup was made of organ meat and herbs. The eggs were the color of blood.

Which was more interesting? It was no contest.

When Lisa was thirty, a brief love affair left her with Anya. Suddenly, she understood her parents' need to make the world better than it really was.

Lisa read her small daughter fairy tale after fairy tale. She poured happy endings into her, like a charm. *Yes, there are bad things in the world*, she wanted to say, *but I will protect you. I will fight for you.*

Anya trusted her. She was proud of her mother, the lawyer, the fighter. Proud of the way she defeated her enemies.

Lisa believed they were an unusually close mother and daughter. Maybe that was an illusion. The first time her daughter stood up to her after twenty years, the first time she said no, Lisa betrayed her.

CHAPTER 3

A Snake in Paradise

Just after Ventura, the road turned east, away from the ocean. Lisa headed toward the mountains. Before long, she reached Ojai.

The mountains surrounded Ojai like a wall. The orchards filled the valley and stretched up the slopes. They looked like a patchwork shawl on the valley's shoulders. Lines of citrus trees formed squares that crisscrossed each other. Bright oranges and lemons speckled the dark green leaves.

Below the groves rested the little town. It looked like a postcard of

California with its red-tile roofs and white-walled houses, its lush gardens.

The locals guarded Ojai's charm like a treasure. No big buildings, no chain stores or malls were allowed.

Her grandfather used to say: "It's no surprise that when they wanted to film paradise, the motion pictures chose Ojai."

But every paradise has its snake, Lisa thought. As the road turned toward Santa Paula, she spied a large sign. It was for her cousin Ari's garden center.

Ari. Lisa was Joe and Anna's first grandchild, but Ari was the first grand-*son*. He and Lisa had been fighting for attention all their lives. Now they were heading for a crash.

Ari's business was on the road that led to their grandfather's orchard. He lived in Ojai. His mother had moved there to be close to her parents. Lisa was jealous of her cousin. He was close to the land. He was even an expert on trees.

But Lisa knew things about land, too. She was a real estate lawyer. She understood value. As the oldest granddaughter, above all, she understood jam.

Her grandfather's birthday fell in June. This was the season of ripe apricots. When Lisa was a child, her grandmother would cook the fruit into jam. She put the trays of cooked fruit in the sun for a week. Then, when her family arrived, she asked the girls to help put the jam in jars. She taught them how to make it. In those days, everyone went home with jam in their suitcases.

After Lisa's grandmother died, Ari wanted them to sell the land. He thought Joe should move to a home. Lisa said no. Where could the family gather? Most of the cousins in Lisa's generation had young children. They wanted to bring their own families to the orchard. They were also worried about the responsibility. None of them were ready to face the choice between selling and keeping. At ninety, Joe was still strong.

They'd pledged to share the financial costs of the upkeep, for as long as it took. Ari said he would look after the orchard.

Lisa's father was dead. So was Ari's mother. The great-grandchildren were growing up. Some years only Lisa, Anya, and two of Lisa's aunts were there to make the jam.

Joe was turning one hundred. More of the family was coming than had been together in a decade. Ari had sent e-mails telling them it was time to sell.

Lisa was ready for another fight. But she was arriving without Anya— her strongest ally and her best defense.

CHAPTER 4

Arrival

FRIDAY EVENING

When she pulled into the driveway, Lisa counted four cars already: her two aunts' small hatchbacks and her brother John's BMW. John was staying at the expensive Valley Inn, but he'd promised Lisa he'd be around as much as possible. Ari's truck was nowhere to be seen.

The car clicked as it cooled down. Lisa opened the trunk.

The jars she'd brought to make the jam sat in a box. The drive had not damaged the glass. She felt happy to see the jars in their rows. They looked like soldiers, lined shoulder to shoulder and topped with tin caps.

Lizards slithered off the rocks as Lisa walked toward the porch. She headed around the back, toward the rusty screen of the kitchen door. No one used the formal front door, with its bell for strangers.

There they were, in the shade: four wooden boxes brimming with golden globes of apricots. Ari had warned her it was getting harder and harder to get good fruit from the old trees. But these looked beautiful to her.

Lisa picked up an apricot and held it against her nose. It smelled like her grandmother. It smelled like childhood. She bit into the fruit. It was sweet, with a tang of sour. Just right.

Lisa was reaching for another globe when her finger skimmed the edge of the box. A small splinter went under her skin.

She swore. Then she blamed her cousin. The boxes had been provided by Ari. So this was all his fault.

CHAPTER 5

In the Kitchen

Her grandmother's kitchen had not changed since Lisa was a child. It was lined with wooden cabinets, painted bright yellow. The counter was made of stone. Lisa remembered it as white, but it was gray now.

In the middle was an island with stools around it. On two perched her aunts: Deena and Susan. They were the "girls"—the two youngest of the four children and the last two still alive.

"Welcome, welcome darling. You look wonderful. Put your bag on the floor and have some tea with us," said Deena.

Lisa's aunt Deena was small and round. Her cheeks were extra large because she was always smiling. She had only recently retired as an elementary teacher. Her students loved her so much they sent her Christmas cards years later.

"I've got to run my hand under water. I got a splinter from Ari's boxes!" said Lisa.

Lisa saw Deena look at Susan, who frowned.

"Where's Anya?" Susan sounded sharp. Susan taught high school. She never got cards.

Lisa turned her back as she went to the sink. "You know how it is with kids. They make their own plans."

Lisa thought it was easier to lie by telling part of the truth.

"Do you think there's some tweezers here?"

The aunts went over the list of who had arrived and who was still coming. They talked about the menu. Tonight they would have something easy: steaks, a pasta salad. Tomorrow would be the big feast. Everyone was making or bringing something. The aunts brought filo dough to roll the spinach pastries called *bureki*.

"I'll do the jam in the morning," said Lisa.

"Oh, the jam, darling. Are we doing the jam this year?"

"Yes! I brought the jars. Ari's picked the fruit. I've told everyone to make sure they are here by nine to do the prep. We'll clear the kitchen by lunchtime."

"I hope Anya will make it. She's so good at organizing the little ones."

"Well, they're all getting bigger now."

"Okay, honey." Deena seemed happy. "You've got the back room."

Susan gave her a high school teacher's look: *I know you are hiding something.*

"Check the sheets are still okay before you put them on the bed. Give them a good shake. I'm afraid we've got mice. We should all be in the hotel like your brother. This house is so old and dry, one spark and *whoosh*. Like Ari says—" Susan's instructions were interrupted.

"Ari!" Lisa put down her mug. She opened her mouth, but Deena jumped in.

"Let's not start that now."

Lisa drained the last of her tea. "Where's Pappou?"

"Pappou's in the living room. The nurse is with him."

CHAPTER 6

Old Hands

Lisa's grandfather was small in his large chair. The nurse sat next to him, typing on her laptop. Someone had dressed him in a clean baby-blue shirt with a turquoise-topped bolero tie. He still had a thick, rich cap of white hair. His eyes were closed, but when Lisa took his hand, he looked up at her. His eyes were sharp as ever.

She kissed his fingers. "Happy birthday."

He smiled back. "Not till tomorrow."

Did he even know who she was?

"It's Lisa," she said.

"I know that, darling."

His fingers squeezed hers. His voice was scratchy, low. It still kept a slight lilt from his Greek, the rolling *r*'s of the immigrant. "Where's your girl?"

She could not lie to him.

"We had a little fight." She dropped her voice. "I'm sure she'll be here."

She did not know if he heard her. She kissed his hand again. His veins were knotted like purple roots. His fingers, though, gripped hers. Still strong. His electrician's hands. His magic hands.

Her grandfather had been born as Iosef, in another century. The name meant "he who adds." He had never stopped adding. He was quick and

smart, keeping ahead of death. Even at
a hundred, he was not ready to give up.
He was paying attention.

CHAPTER 7

Almost a Full House

By early evening, the house felt full. There were ten adults and eight children, ranging from newborn Abe, Deena's latest grandchild, to Joe. Lisa's brother, John, drove from Seattle. Her cousin Becky flew in from Phoenix. Others had come from their homes in towns nearby. Some members of the New York branch stayed home. Also missing were Lisa's daughter and her mother, Claire, who was in Florida.

Lisa tried to lose herself in the pleasure of the gathering. The sound of so many relatives in one place was like a childhood song. Lisa listened for familiar notes: the clap of the refrigerator door; the clink of ice in glasses; the mix of voices, male and female, high and low. Over and under, a train of children whistled through the house.

That first night, they ate informally. Lisa sat at the outdoor table with her grandfather and some of the mothers and children. Their little heads echoed each other: dark curls in different sizes.

They ate from the giant bowl of pasta salad she had helped her aunts make. It was child-friendly, but still different. They had reworked the familiar American dish by adding olive oil, feta cheese, and fresh oregano from the garden.

If this were the last gathering in this house, would the children remember the taste of their great-grandmother's garden?

Lisa had brought a large leg of lamb in a cooler. It was now in the fridge. She had been marinating it in olive oil, lemon, wine, rosemary, and oregano. At noon, twenty-four hours after starting the marinade, Lisa would cook the roast. She would add the garlic as whole cloves. She would make slits in the flesh with a knife, like her father taught her.

After three hours of roasting, the meat would fall off the bone. She would put the potatoes right in the pot, too. They always came out oily and crunchy on the outside, and soft on the inside. No one could resist her father's recipe for lamb.

In Lisa's family, her mother had

done most of the cooking, but sometimes her father cooked on Sundays. Jack had remained Greek in his cooking. He always made his mother's recipes.

His food was so different from the typical North American fare they ate during the week: tuna bakes with melted cheese, hot dogs in white buns, iceberg lettuce covered in ranch dressing. As children, Lisa and her brother took their father's efforts for granted. Sometimes, they even complained about the foreign flavor.

When Lisa grew up, she appreciated his genius. At dinner parties, she cooked like Jack. Her guests always praised the food. She looked exotic, her hair dark and curly and wild. She wore gold hoop earrings, like all her aunts. She collected Greek folk music and played it for her guests.

Her parents might have tried to hide their roots, but Lisa celebrated and shared her ethnic heritage. It was a big part of her identity.

CHAPTER 8

In the Orchard

After dinner, the air was cooler, and Lisa announced she was going for a walk. She put her phone in her pocket and stepped out from the porch and into the orchard.

The trees, which had seemed so large to her as a child, now looked small and ancient. But Ari had kept them trimmed, she could see that, and their tops were well rounded. They looked like children's drawings of trees: round tops, straight trunks.

The winter had been wet, and the grass was still green in the shade. Lisa could feel old leaves and pits from last season crunching under her feet.

When Lisa was a child, her grandfather told her that the health of the orchard started here: in the grass. He'd kept it cut short, free from insects and invaders.

"Healthy soil makes healthy trees," Joe would say.

This evening, the growth was thick as a jungle. Ari did not have time to mow. She could see the tall grass was dotted here and there with fallen fruit. Up close, she saw the results, too. Some of the leaves on the trees were speckled with blight.

Lisa picked up a piece of fruit from the ground. One side was smooth, soft, with a blush of red. The other side had been eaten by an animal or insects, exposing orange flesh and the hard brown stone.

Lisa's grandfather had told her you could always tell where the apricots faced the sun by the blush on their cheeks.

Lisa headed downhill, toward the creek. She could hear children's voices through the rows. The sound brought back a memory from her childhood: her brother and cousins in the creek bed, hunting frogs, whittling sticks with their army knives. Lisa used to pass them and head up the hill at the back of the orchard with her book. She would climb up to the first ridge. She liked to look over the tops of the trees, to listen to them talking to each other.

The wind in their leaves sounded like voices.

The creek was dry. Her cousins' children were there, climbing over the boulders. Lisa smiled at them. They smiled back shyly. She had only met them once before, at her grandfather's ninetieth birthday. They had been too young then to leap around.

Lisa was wearing her sturdy shoes. She started climbing toward her well-loved spot, up and up. Finally, she reached the ridge she remembered.

The day had been so clear. Now, at sunset, a thin line of orange-yellow rested just on top of the horizon. The blue sky above it held a crescent moon. Overhead, deeper blue hinted of the coming night. Shadows surrounded the trees like pools of dark water. At the tips of the shiny leaves, the last sun caught fire.

Lisa sat on a rock. She knew you could get good mobile reception here. In the house, they still relied on a single landline. She tried Anya's number. The phone rang and rang.

From here the orchard looked like a lawn, striped dark and light green. It was hard to see the problem at first. But a few trees had died already. The brown outlines of their branches were like arms reaching out for help.

In her family, too, were patches of brown. Her grandmother, her father, Ari's mother—Lisa's sweet aunt Helen—were all missing from their rows.

Lisa hated that she could not keep them all together forever, safe and sound. She disliked change from an early age. Her family felt like a strong tree that had sprung from one fragile root. Her grandparents had escaped death and fallen in love. They had come to America, and their desire for life had created so much.

And now? Would it all be lost again? She wanted her family to be like an unbroken row, going on and on.

But who was she? A hero, or a hypocrite? Lisa had a chance to add new growth, but instead, she brought blight.

CHAPTER 9

Ghosts

When she was a child, Lisa had followed her grandparents around the house, where they never seemed to sit still. Joe had had his own business. He sold it to a big electronics company for a lot of money during the postwar California boom. That had not slowed him down for a moment. He transferred his work from office to orchard.

Lisa's memories of Joe in those years were of handing him tools while he fixed something: a broken pipe, a ceiling light, a door handle, or a diseased tree. Her grandmother did not stay still either. There were stools in the kitchen, but she never used them. She moved back and forth between the sink, the oven, and the counter without resting. If she was not in the kitchen, she was in her walled garden, tending her herbs and tomatoes.

Joe only told his grandchildren happy stories.

"I was so small and pretty as a boy, I looked just like a girl. So they smuggled me away wearing my sisters' skirts and my mother's headscarf. And what with this and with that, I never grew. And then I got to Thessaloniki, and there in the tent next to mine was your grandmother. And you know what happened? I started eating like nobody's business. I grew straight up: six inches in six months. She fell in love with me.

She followed me to America and now, here we are!"

All of his stories ended the same way: *here we are!*

Like the story of how he came to buy the orchard.

"I got my first job here in the motion pictures, fixing lights. No one else wanted to do it. They were all scared of the electricity. It wasn't much money in the beginning, but we got tickets to everything. I liked to take the kids, give their mother a break. This particular film was by Frank Capra. You know Capra was an immigrant like me, from Sicily? Once we talked about growing oranges.

"So what happens in the movie? A group of people gets lost in the mountains. It's snowing, terrible, they almost die, but then—then they stumble on a hidden valley. A paradise. Full of flowers and beautiful, happy people. Everyone's welcoming. They find out that the guy who runs the valley has discovered the secret of long life. People live for hundreds of years, but they can't leave. So they decide to escape and take this beautiful girl with them, to tell the world.

"Guess what happens? As soon as she hits the snow, she ages three hundred years. In a minute! She turns to dust and blows away! And there were my kids, sobbing. And me? I'm laughing! You know why? Because God bless America, they are crying at make-believe, at a girl who goes up in a puff of smoke, then gets up a minute later to light her cigarette and flirt with the cameraman.

"The valley, I found out, was real. It was all filmed here in Ojai. As soon as I got a chance, I came here to see it for myself. And now: *here we are!*"

Lisa's grandfather's stories hinted at dark things but always had happy endings. They were refugees, but they fell in love! They arrived in America without a penny, but they found help on the first day! Their distant cousin invited them to California and they took the train! On his very first job, Joe discovered he was an electrical genius!

No one talked about what happened before. No details of how they became

orphans were given. Lisa was left thinking: What if the girl didn't walk off set
and smoke a cigarette? What if she
were someone you knew? Someone you
loved? What if she were real?

CHAPTER 10

Insomnia

While everyone slept, Lisa lay in bed and made another phone call. The weak cell signal was better at this late hour, but she hung up without leaving a message when it went to voicemail. How could Anya not call her back? How long would her daughter punish her? Was Anya really going to make Lisa face the jam-making on her own?

Her aunt Susan was right. It was hot in the house. The walls felt like tinder.

Lisa pushed the thin sheet off her body. She sat up in the dark and wrapped her arms around her legs. She thought about getting a glass of water, but she did not move. Ever since she'd come upon her grandmother one night in the kitchen when she was ten, she did not like to cross the dark house.

One June night many years ago, Lisa had been visiting the orchard with her family. That morning they had made the jam. At midnight, everyone was asleep except Lisa.

It was hot and she wanted water. She walked through the dark house. The kitchen light was on. There, she found her grandmother, also awake. She was sitting on a stool for once. On the counter next to her was a jar of jam, open. In her hand, she held a spoon. Tears poured down her cheeks.

Lisa crept closer. She put her arms around her grandmother's waist. Her grandmother pulled Lisa's head against her body. She stroked Lisa's hair. For a time, all Lisa heard was the sound of Anna's breathing as she calmed herself.

Then she pulled Lisa onto a stool. She offered her a bowl of yogurt and jam. They ate quietly together, Anna spooning jam right out of the jar.

Maybe it was the way the quiet of the night put them on an island, alone together. Maybe it was the taste of the jam that unlocked Anna's tongue. For whatever reason, she told her secret to Lisa. She told her why she made the jam. Even though she never spoke about it again, Lisa remembered the story all her life.

"In my village, we all lived together. Greeks, Armenians, Jews. That's what it was like under the Ottomans. We were all under the same thumb.

"Then somebody got the idea: Turks for the Turks. Greeks for the Greeks. Everybody out. We heard about it, but it was like a distant, crazy fight that had nothing to do with us.

"My best friend was a little Armenian girl. We did everything together. Her mother was the one who taught me how to put the jam in the sun. We used to help her. Every house had its own trees. In the spring they gave us flowers. In the summer, fruit. You only had to reach up, and there were apricots like honey. So sweet."

Anna sucked the fruit off the spoon. She closed her eyes. Then, slowly, carefully, she put the spoon down and dropped her head, holding it in her palms like it was going to drop. She looked up. Was she even seeing Lisa? For years afterward, Lisa wondered.

"Do you know why I am alive today and my little Armenian friend is not? Because I was sick. Because I had a fever. My mother sent me to her sister in another village to protect the others from infection.

"I wasn't there when the bad men came. They were not from our area; they were strangers. I heard later the government picked ones who enjoyed killing and sent them to the villages. They rounded up the Christians and put them in a church. I did not see, but I heard how they locked the door and lit the fire.

Her grandmother's eyes were wide. "I was your age. I never saw my mother again. In the middle of the night, we ran. We knew they were coming for us. My aunt died on the boat. Lots of people did. We threw their bodies over the sides for the sharks.

"I could never go back to Turkey. Everything about it was dead. Me too. Dead, dead, dead. Then I met Joe. Oh boy, then I wanted to live.

"We came to America. We came here. I saw the trees. Blossoms so white, honey, so beautiful and alive. I knew

I wanted to make the jam again. To bring back the ones I lost. To feel them with me, every year."

Lisa put her arms around her grandmother again. Anna's body felt so soft: real and breathing. It might never have been and then she, too, would never have been.

Her grandmother broke the spell of the ghosts.

"You like the jam, don't you?" She pulled Lisa's hair back from her wet face.

Lisa never said a word. She only nodded.

"Finish it, honey. Don't waste a drop."

Lisa scraped her bowl with her spoon until every drop was gone.

"You're gonna remember the recipe?"

Lisa nodded again.

"Good girl!" Her grandmother had slid off her stool, taking the bowl with her. She screwed the lid back on the jam.

"Don't tell anyone else this story, darling. I don't like to talk about it. Like Joe says, what's the use? What good can it do? After all, *here we are.*"

Lisa had never told anyone her grandmother's story, but she thought about it every year. She had decided to share the story with Anya this year.

Her plans were interrupted by a phone call.

CHAPTER 11

On the Phone

TWO WEEKS EARLIER

"I'm in love!"

It was Anya calling from her apartment in Berkeley.

Lisa was shocked. Anya was so private. She'd had small crushes and a few dates, but Lisa had never heard this tone in her voice before.

Lisa asked the obvious questions.

"How did you meet?"

"In a class on grafting. Isn't that funny? Biology 311: Roots and Shoots."

"Where's he from?"

"Here. He grew up in Berkeley. He's a total Northern Californian."

"Really. What's his name?"

"Edi."

"Eddy? That's a nice name. Old-fashioned."

"It's really Edil. We both changed our names when we were kids. Remember when I became Anne? But he never changed back to Edil."

"Edil? E-d-i-l? Unusual. Where's it from?"

Anya hesitated for only a moment. "His parents are Turkish."

"Turkish! Oh."

Here Lisa could still have turned back. She could have made a different choice. But she did not stop.

"We've had all kinds of Christians in our family, and your cousin Barbara married a Jewish man. But this Edil is Turkish, you said? What kind of Turkish? Muslim Turkish?"

"He says he's not religious. Neither am I."

"But he knows about how your grandparents were kicked out of Turkey?"

"Mom! All of that happened a long time ago. I want to bring him to the reunion. I'm sure no one cares about that old stuff."

"Hmn." Lisa made a noise, neither yes nor no.

"He's going to be the most important person in my life. I want him to see the orchard. Ari says next year it won't be there."

A red heat rose inside Lisa. Before she knew what she was saying, the words came out of her mouth. "Actually, honey, I don't think it *is* a good idea to bring this new Turkish boyfriend to your grandfather's hundredth birthday. I think *I* mind."

"Are you kidding?"

"No!"

Soon they were shouting at each other. Lisa lost all reason. In the middle of a rant about how everyone was against her, Anya hung up the phone. For twenty years, Lisa had spoken to her daughter nearly every day. The silence between them was now more than two weeks old, and it was killing Lisa.

CHAPTER 12

Talking and Not Talking

SATURDAY MORNING

Lisa woke up at dawn. The house was quiet. She put on her running shoes. First she went back to the ridge and tried Anya again. Then she ran off her frustration on the empty road. By the time she'd finished, the children had woken their parents, and her brother and sister-in-law had arrived with a big bag of croissants from town.

The day before, she'd avoided meeting Ari face to face. He was there now, working the barbecue, talking to the cousins, chasing his wild sons. He nodded at her across the crowd.

After breakfast, Lisa asked the kids to help her lift the jars out of the back of the car. She told them how they were going to sterilize them in the oven. First they needed a wash. The kids loved the bubbles and the water. By the time they finished, the kitchen floor was slippery enough to slide across.

There was a long table in the garden where Lisa set up the stations. Each child was given two bowls: one for the fruit, one for the pits. Their knives were not too sharp. There was no need; the fruit was ripe and parted easily.

She got the teenagers to fill two big pots with water to put in the middle of the table to rinse the apricots.

It was a warm morning. The children liked the water. They liked the knives. But Lisa knew their attention was limited. This generation of screen watchers never stuck with anything for long. The sun was already warm overhead.

Soon they started splashing each other.

"Settle down! Watch out!" called Lisa.

At that moment, Ari's youngest son tipped a vat of water over. A waterfall poured off the wooden table and pooled on the Spanish tiles.

"Where's Ari?" Lisa's voice was sharp. "He's got to control these kids. Ari!"

As if by magic, Ari appeared. He lifted the boy by his armpits and swung him into the air.

"What are you doing? Eh, you rascal!" He was smiling, and the boy laughed.

"Lisa, they're bored. I told you. If you want to do this, go ahead, but you can't count on the children. They run out of patience." He put his son on the ground and playfully swatted him. "Go play. Leave your aunt in peace."

"Now I've lost a worker," Lisa grumbled. But to her surprise, Ari straddled the bench and took his son's place.

"Let me help a few minutes."

Ari's hands were large, like their grandfather's. The little knife looked like a toy in his fingers. He wore his usual clean green polo shirt and khaki trousers. His enormous feet looked twice as large in his work boots. Ari looked like a boss, but a boss who was not afraid to get his hands dirty.

"I thought Anya was supposed to be here to help. That's what she told me."

"What? When?" Lisa felt the sharp edge of an apricot stone along her thumb.

"Yesterday."

"You spoke to her yesterday?"

"Yes, didn't you?"

"I need to refill this vat your son spilled." Lisa went over to the hose. Already the sun was drying the puddle the water had made. Lisa let the water run slowly while she thought about what to say.

She was not ready to admit to Ari that she and Anya were not speaking. She was jealous, again, of her cousin. Ari and Anya were close. They shared a passion for growing things. They were both practical, quiet people. Lisa felt like a crashing elephant around them.

She only knew one way to be.

"I want to talk to you about the orchard, Ari."

"Sure. We all need to talk. What about later? Before dinner."

"Deena and Susan said they wanted us to make the decision. It's our future."

"The future is obvious. We can't preserve this place like a museum. Someone has to invest in the land. They need to make it work again, to sell the fruit."

"Why don't you sell the fruit?"

"I've got my own business, Lisa! I'm busy! Everyone is."

"We have to think harder."

"Think all you want! The trees don't think. They just live or die."

Her brother John caught her eye. He gave her that look she knew so well, the one that said, *Please, please, don't make trouble.*

The children had stopped working. They were looking at their elders.

Lisa took a breath. John jumped in with his cheerful voice.

"Come on, kids, let's help your aunt make jam!" Oh, he was just like their parents, avoiding trouble!

Her brother played tennis every morning. He was still wearing his whites. His surgeon's hands carefully pared the fruit without getting anything on his clothes. He looked so calm and elegant.

Lisa's hands were shaking. She grabbed a piece of fruit and dipped it in the cold water. She cut into the soft globe. Inside, the flesh was the color of a sunset on a clear day. The hard pit was wet and dark brown, like earth, and sharp on the edges.

She did not see Ari get up from the table, but she heard him.

The sun rose higher, but the arbor gave them shade. The old grapevine curled over their heads. Lisa's breath calmed. She lost herself in her labor. As she worked, she felt the tendrils of the grapevine twisting and growing, binding together all the people underneath—and all their history, too.

CHAPTER 13

Making Jam

By the time they got to the kitchen, they were down to a small crew: Lisa, her aunts, Ari's sister, and John's wife, Gwen. Just the women. The workers.

They took the vats of water off the table and cleaned them. Then they filled each one with fruit. They placed them on opposite corners of the stove, above a low flame. Lisa pulled out the bags of sugar she had bought. She poured an equal measure in each pot.

"Do you have to use pectin?" Gwen asked. "When we made fruit jam as kids we always used pectin. But ours never set right: too runny or too hard."

"Apricots have their own natural pectin," said Lisa. "Just watch."

In fifteen minutes, the flesh had broken down into a swirling sea of orange. Small bubbles rose up in the liquid. Lisa stirred the pot to keep the mixture from sticking to the bottom of the pot. She turned off the heat.

"Okay everybody, we need to do this fast."

The jars had been set on the table earlier. Lisa lifted the vats of cooked jam off the hob and put them on the table. With big spoons, the women lifted up the hot fruit. They poured it through funnels into the jars. Soon the sticky orange was everywhere: on the table, on their fingers, in their hair. They talked as they worked. They laughed at themselves.

Each jar was sealed with a rubber ring, making a satisfying click.

Lisa needed this. All year long, she fought alone—for her clients, against her enemies. This physical labor with family was deeply relaxing. She felt her grandmother next to her, and her father, too, and all the others she had never known. Even if her jam was lighter than her grandmother's, it was beautiful in the glass, a golden harvest.

At last, the final jar was sealed. The glass was still hot. The jam would take time to cool and set. Meanwhile, they cleaned the kitchen to get ready for the next stage. Lisa wanted to put the lamb on and then go lie down.

She had not slept much last night, and she would need all her energy for whatever surprises lay ahead.

CHAPTER 14

Talking, At Last

Saturday Afternoon

The jars had cooled. Lisa had cleaned them and put them on the sideboard in the dining room. Later, she would give them to her cousins.

She knew she could find Ari in the orchard. He was down by the creek, where he used to chase frogs as a boy.

He could hear her crunching as she approached.

"I want to show you something," he said, and leaned down and pushed through the grass. The soil he picked up crumbled between his fingers. "It's not just the fruit, Lisa. Water costs money. So does security. Last year one of my workers found a camp of hippies who'd parked on the back lawn. They broke down the fence. We had to chase them away."

"You keep talking about how much everything costs, but there is something here you can't put a price on," said Lisa. "Something I'm willing to fight for."

"This isn't only about the money. Land needs to be worked."

"What if we leased the orchard?"

"Look, even you don't have time anymore. You show up once a year to make jam. You can buy it in the shop!"

"It's not the jam. It's the making it that counts. Picking the fruit, harvesting it, keeping it. It's all a link to Anna, from her to us to our children. Do we have a right to break that link?"

"Well, your daughter is the oldest grandchild. She agrees with me."

Lisa felt a sharp pain under her ribs.

"How do you know that?"

"She told me. She can tell you herself. She's arriving soon. With her Turkish boyfriend."

It was like a relapse after you think you have recovered. Once again, Lisa lost her head to rage.

"Do you know how many messages I've left her? I've tried to reach her a hundred times a day and she won't call me back, but somehow you know everything! She's my daughter, Ari! My daughter!"

Her voice rose to a screech. The wind caught it and flung it higher. Lisa wanted to run. Where could she go? She needed to be alone.

She turned her back to Ari. She headed toward her ridge. Ari called, but she did not turn around.

Her brother, John, found her on a rock, curled over with her head on her knees. He was a good listener, for a surgeon. He waited while she cried. Then he made her laugh.

Finally, she told him the story of her fights with Anya and Ari.

"I see," her brother said quietly, like a doctor thinking of his diagnosis.

"I don't even really care that he's a Turk."

"His *parents* are Turkish. He's an American."

"I know. I know."

"What do you think *really* upset you?"

John was the father of twin girls, both at college on the East Coast. He knew how to talk to women: to ask questions and to wait for the answers.

"It was the way she sprang it on me." Lisa took a small stone she had been holding in her palm and threw it. "Anya's never had a serious boyfriend before. I always thought she would tell me everything. The first date. The first kiss. But I don't hear a word until it's already, 'We're in love. We want to meet each other's families.'"

"So you overreacted."

"I reacted! Okay, I overreacted."

"You've always had a temper."

"I have?"

"Yes. You terrified me as a kid. You still scare me a bit."

Lisa laughed. "But I'm such a softie! Just because I don't like to admit I'm wrong . . ."

Lisa wiped her hands on her jeans and continued. "John, let me ask you: am I wrong this time? I can't tell you how much I hate the thought of losing this place. All our connections. I hate change."

"Everything comes to an end, Lisa. Good things and bad."

They sat together quietly for a few minutes before John put his hand on her back. "You can keep making jam for everyone," he said.

"No, this will be the last time. I can keep telling stories. You don't need an orchard for that."

CHAPTER 15

Branches from the Same Root

Lisa and John were nearly back at the house when they heard a car pull into the driveway.

"Oh, John, I don't think I can face them. What will I say?"

"Sometimes I find it is better not to say anything."

"I've never tried that!"

But she did. She walked out to greet her daughter and she opened her arms. First she held Anya and kissed her. Then she hugged Edi. From the way he sprang back, she could see Anya had warned him.

"I'm giving you my room. I'll sleep up in the loft with the kids."

He softened and smiled. "Thanks!"

"You don't have to do that, Mom," said Anya. "We'll sleep in the loft."

"Really?" asked Lisa.

Edi grabbed his backpack. "Sure! I love camping out."

As Anya locked the car, Edi turned to Lisa. "You know, I'm so excited to be here. I can't believe Anya's great-granddad is a hundred! That's like, whoa."

Anya was right. He had a nice smile. His hair was dark and curly like her daughter's. Like Anya, when he spoke, he sounded like a Californian, like a surfer, like a dude. He sounded like a visitor from a future none of them had yet imagined.

In the evening, Anya and Lisa walked out into the orchard. The smell of smoke from the grill drifted between the trunks. A dove sat on a branch, sending out its sad and sweet *hello*s.

"I'm sorry," Lisa started.

"I'm sorry, too, Mom."

"Please don't do that to me again. I don't care how mad you are."

"I felt so hurt. I never thought you'd say don't come."

"I said don't come with your boyfriend! I was wrong. I don't care if you go out with an axe murderer, you're still my daughter."

"Edi's not an axe murderer!"

"No, he's a sweet boy. And Pappou likes him."

As they walked, the wind stirred in

the leaves. A few wasps hunted in the fallen fruit. The trees rested, waiting. In the spring, they would flower again. Bees would return. Small apricot buds would ripen again in the sun.

"I'll miss this place so much, Mom."

Lisa tried to smile through her tears. "At least you're here now."

Anya was a full head taller than her mother. She rested her chin on Lisa's curls. Around them, the trees watched. Their branches full of leaves looked like arms holding green baskets.

"Shall we go back?" Lisa was the first to move.

"Edi and I have been talking, Mom. Maybe we can both come here to help with the trees. He has a lot of ideas. You know, if we're still together."

"Is that right? But Ari said you agreed with him!"

"I did. But now, I think maybe there's a way."

"I never thought I'd say this, darling, but I don't mind. You mean more to me than any tree. Whatever you decide, I'll back you up."

CHAPTER 16

The Birthday Dinner

Edi sat next to Anya at dinner. They looked like twins. They both wore jeans and white tops. His was button-down. Hers was a T-shirt. She wore a necklace with a shell, and so did he. Lisa wondered if they had given those to each other.

Lisa's grandfather sat at the head, under the arbor. On the table was a line of dishes: piles of pastries, the lamb shoulder, chicken baked with apricots and tomatoes, salads, grilled eggplant, potatoes roasted in olive oil, chickpeas with herbs, yogurts, plates of feta cheese, and bowls of olives.

"*Bureki*," Edi said, reaching for the pastries Lisa's aunts had rolled that afternoon. "I love these!"

When he said his mother had a special way of making apricot jam by letting the fruit stew in the pan under the heat of the sun, Lisa started laughing.

"I was going to tell you a story about that," she said, "but instead, I think Joe should tell how he saw this valley in a movie, a long time ago."

Joe looked at her through his watery eyes.

"You tell the story, honey," he said. "My voice ain't so good anymore."

So Lisa told them the story, just like she remembered hearing it so many times. The small children grew quiet and listened. Ari leaned back in his chair and looked up into the sky.

It rose over them, a blue bowl spilling into black, a bowl that was beginning to fill with stars. The wind rustled in the grape arbor. In another year, Lisa thought, this might all be gone. On the other hand, maybe not.

Lisa came to the end of the story.

She repeated her grandfather's words: *"And here we are."*

"Here we are, darling," Joe said, looking at all of them. "Here we are, thank God."

VOCABULARY

Ally: someone on your side in a fight

Armenians: a group of Christians who once lived in Turkey. Between 1915 and 1922, most of the population was forcibly expelled or killed. Other ethnic groups targeted were the Greeks and the Assyrians.

Bolero tie: also known as a bolo tie; a kind of thin rope necktie common in the American West, often held with a silver or turquoise clasp

Ethnic cleansing: genocide, the

mass killing of one group of
people by another

Frank Capra: a film director
famous in the 1930s and 1940s

Funnel: a hollow kitchen aid
that is wide at the top and
narrow at the bottom; good for
transferring jam from a large
pot to a smaller jar

Grafting: the process of taking
a branch from one tree and
adding it to another to make
new growth

Greeks: a Mediterranean nation
of people with ancient roots,
mostly Orthodox Christian

Jackson Browne: a rock singer
from the 1970s

Loft: a part of a house that is above

the ceiling, often opened up to use for sleeping

Orchard: a group of trees farmed to produce fruit

The Ottoman Empire: an empire founded in Turkey in the fourteenth century that lasted until the First World War. At its height, it controlled much of the Eastern Mediterranean and large parts of the Middle East.

Pectin: a natural gelling agent that occurs in fruit and keeps it from getting runny

Turks: a Mediterranean nation of people with ancient roots, mostly Muslim

UCLA: the University of California in Los Angeles

Food names:

Bureki: a Turkish pastry of stuffed
filo dough, often filled with feta
and herbs

Feta: a salty goat cheese made in
and near Greece

Filo: a kind of dough that is so
thin it looks like paper

Place names:

Ojai: a small town two hours north
of Los Angeles, known for its
orchards and artists

Seattle, Phoenix: Western
American cities a few hundred
miles from Los Angeles

Sicily: an Italian island in the
Mediterranean

Thessaloniki: a city in northern

Greece which took in many refugees during the period of upheaval after the First World War

Ventura County, Thousand Oaks, Santa Paula: places around Los Angeles on the way to Ojai

CPSIA information can be obtained
at www.ICGtesting.com
Printed in the USA
FFOW02n1716170318
45819216-46713FF